GHOUL ON A STOOL
A HALLOWEEN TRADITION

Created by Juan Hernandez

Written by Charity Hernandez

Illustrated by Prosenjit Mondal

www.ghoulonastool.com   First Edition – 2015   Printed in China

Have you ever wondered where your Halloween candy comes from?

The chocolate, the lollipops, and the ooey
gooey gum drops?

The secret has been hidden for thousands of years, now is the time for its big premier!

I am a ghoul, in case you didn't know! I'm small, and green, and no, I don't glow!

I work at a factory with my friends,
sitting on stools until the night ends.

All different candies are what we create,
so you will have lots of choices to make!

Sometimes the candy can be very tempting, so I sneak a piece when my tummy is empty.

My teeth are not the best they can be, so I see
my dentist regularly.

We work for Mr. Can D. Corn and to finish the candy is what we have sworn.

If we finish by October 1st date,we get to come
home with you to your state!

You can name us if you choose.

We love to play,

read books,

or just take a snooze.

My favorite game is hide and seek,
so find me in the morning and try not to peek!

There is one thing that we request …

that you do a good deed, and be kind to the rest,
like saying thank you, or helping someone...

or just being nice and sharing your fun.

But if you are mean I will play a trick to blow
off some steam.

like take your sock so you only have one...

or take your shoe and stick it in some gum.

I might make a mess with all of your toys, so
you will have to clean up all I destroy!

So please be kind and follow our request,
and we'll make sure your Halloween's a success!

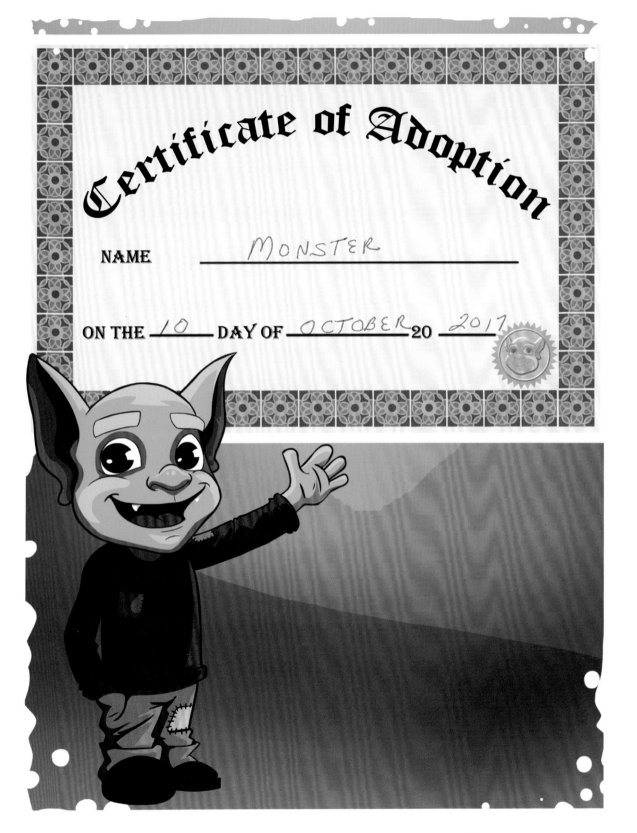

Certificate of Adoption

NAME _MONSTER_

ON THE _10_ DAY OF _OCTOBER_ 20 _2017_

from
GRAM
&
PAP